D1477644

Robot's SPECIAL DAY

Mary Ray

Illustrated by
Tony Sumpter

dingles & company
COMMUNITY LIBRARY NETWORK
AT POST FALLS
821 N SPOKANE STREET
POST FALLS, ID 83854

First published in the United States of America in 2008 by
dingles & company
P.O. Box 508
Sea Girt, New Jersey 08750

First Printing

Website: www.dingles.com
E-mail: info@dingles.com

Library of Congress Catalog Card Number
2007906325

ISBN
978-1-59646-960-0 (library binding)
978-1-59646-961-7 (paperback)

Robot's Special Day
Text © Mary Ray, 2003
This U.S. edition of *Robot's Special Day*, originally published in English
in 2007, is published by arrangement with Oxford University Press.

The moral rights of the author have been asserted.
Database right Oxford University Press (maker).

Printed in China

Contents

cloud

weather

rain

rainbow

Chapter *1*

Robot Gets a Job

The only space was next to Chelsea Carter. Robot didn't want to sit next to Chelsea Carter.

"Sit down, Robot," said his teacher, Miss Turner.

Robot's real name was Robert. But when he was little, he couldn't say "Robert" properly. So he ended up as Robot. And now that's what most people called him.

He sat down.

"We've got a special visitor today," said Miss Turner. "The Mayor's coming to see us!" She gave her warning look. "So you'll all be good, won't you?"

Robot felt as if she meant just him. Chelsea Carter smiled. She thought she was always good.

Miss Turner began to call the register.

Robot thought about the visit. A
mayor sounded important. Like a king.
Only with a gold chain instead of
a crown. And a big car.

Chelsea Carter pushed Robot hard.
"Wake up! You've got to say 'Yes,
Miss Turner.'"

"That's enough Chelsea," said Miss
Turner. "Leave Robot alone."

That told her, thought Robot. He
smiled at Miss Turner. Miss Turner
smiled back.

"I need someone to take the register.
Will you do it, Robot?"

Robot could hardly believe his ears. She was asking him to take the register to the office!

Chelsea Carter couldn't believe her ears either.

"I could go with him."

"No," said Miss Turner." This job is for Robot."

She handed him the register.

An important job! On his own!

Robot beamed.

Chapter *2*

Where Is Everyone?

"Straight there and straight back," said Miss Turner.

Robot set off. He loved helping. It was easier than writing and number work. Mostly, he never got chosen. He'd never had an important job.

In the hall, Mrs. Peters' class was gathered around the piano. Robot tiptoed carefully. His sneakers squeaked.

"Robert Weston!" barked Mrs Peters. "Stop making noise in my class!"

It wasn't fair! He hadn't made noise.

Robot went through to the entrance hall. There was no one there. Just the fish, drifting round their tank.

The principal's room was empty. So was Mrs. Gohill's office. It was spooky. Where was everybody?

Robot put the register on Mrs. Gohill's desk. On her computer, a spaceship turned slowly. Robot gazed at it. He'd like one of those. And a telephone. And a special tray for paper clips and pens.

Robot suddenly felt scared. He shouldn't be there on his own. What if Mrs. Mason, the principal, found him? He'd get told off! He dashed out of the office.

Robot skidded to a halt in the entrance hall. A lady and a man were by the fish tank. They were all dressed up – and had on enormous gold chains.

Chapter 3

A Good Idea

"Hello," said the lady. "We wondered where everyone was. Let me guess. You're the caretaker."

Robot grinned. "She comes after school."

"You must be the principal, then!" said the lady.

Robot giggled. "No! I'm Robot."

The lady laughed. "Wonderful! A school run by a robot!" And she shook Robot's hand.

Robot tried to look grown up. But he didn't know what to say. She looked like his aunt. Except for the chain.

He never had important visitors at home. Just people like Mrs. Went from next door and his aunt. They were always dropping in to visit.

Suddenly, he knew what to do.
"Would you like some tea?"
he asked.

"That would be wonderful!" said the lady. "You show us the way."

In the big hall, Mrs. Peters was playing the piano. Robot put a finger to his lips.

"We mustn't make a noise," he whispered. "Or Mrs. Peters will tell us off."

He walked in time to the music, with his head up. Chelsea Carter had never had a job as important as this! The Mayors followed him.

In Robot's classroom, Miss Turner had her back to the door.

Robot went straight to the Home Corner.

Just then, Chelsea Carter shouted in her "I'm-telling" voice, "Miss Turner! Robert Weston's got two Mayors!"

Miss Turner spun round.
The lady Mayor smiled.

"I hope you were expecting us? Robot asked if we'd like some tea."

She squeezed into the Home Corner
and perched on a chair.

"I'm dying for a cup."

"Are you sure?" asked Miss Turner.

"Certain," said the lady Mayor.

And she told the man to sit down, too.

Chapter 4

"At Home"

Robot dived into the cupboard. He found a teapot with no lid. He also found two saucers, a mug, and a cup with a chewed handle.

Chelsea Carter pushed him out of the way. "You need the table cloth, silly." Chelsea Carter thought she was more important than anyone else in the whole world!

Miss Turner came over.

"Chelsea, Robot can manage." And she led Chelsea Carter back to her seat.

"I've got a teapot like that at home!" said the lady Mayor. "Can I pour?" And she helped Robot make the tea.

Robot found a plastic cake used for number work. And even the man pretended to eat and said, "Mmmm … Delicious."

While they had tea, the lady told Robot about being a Mayor. And the children brought their work to show.

Suddenly Mrs. Mason swept into the class. A man with a camera rushed along behind her.

The whole class stopped.

Mrs. Mason's face was very red! She took the lady Mayor by the hand.

"I'm SO sorry! I didn't know you'd arrived. Then this reporter turned up, and Mrs. Peters told me ..."

Mrs. Mason gave Robot such a look!

"Robot's made us feel SO at home!"
said the lady Mayor. "I think he should
meet all your visitors. It's been our
best visit ever!"

Chapter 5

Famous!

It was Robot's best day ever.

He found out that the lady was the Mayor. The man was her Deputy. Their chains weren't made of real gold. And the Mayors came in a Jaguar with a flag on the hood, and a driver wearing a uniform.

The lady Mayor wanted to have her
picture taken with Robot. It was in
the newspaper:

Hextable Herald

Mayor takes tea with Robot!!

Mayor of Hextable, Maggie Walmsley,
and her Deputy, Reg Todd, had a
surprise welcome when they visited
Hextable Primary School.

The Mayors really enjoyed their visit.
"We met Robot and his friends and
had a lovely tea," said Mrs Walmsley.

The paper told about Robot's name. And it told how much the Mayors enjoyed their visit, too. Miss Turner put it on the wall with a notice saying: "Robot's Special Day!"

And there wasn't a word about Chelsea Carter.

About the author

I'd been trying to write this story for ages, but I couldn't get it right. Then I remembered a boy I used to know, named Robot, who loved helping. And the story fell into place. I don't know anyone named Chelsea. But I've known a few children like her! As for important visitors… It helps if they like children as well as being important.

My husband Tony did the illustrations for the book.

I took this photo in our garden